Peter Pan

Adapted by
Brooke Vitale

Illustrated by the
Disney Storybook Art Team

DISNEP PRESS
Los Angeles • New York

John and Michael Darling
like to play-fight.
They pretend to be
Peter Pan and Captain Hook.

Their sister, Wendy,
puts them to bed.
She tells them a story
about Peter Pan.

Wendy knows that Peter
is a real boy.
She found his shadow
in her room.

Peter comes to listen
to Wendy's story.
She sews his
shadow back on.

Peter wants Wendy to
go to Never Land.
John and Michael
can go, too.

Peter's friend Tinker Bell
gives the children pixie dust.
Now they can fly.

They fly all night long.
In the morning
they see Never Land.

Captain Hook is on his ship.
He does not like Peter Pan.
Peter fed Hook's hand
to a crocodile.

Now the Croc
follows Hook.
It wants to eat
the rest of him.

Hook sees Peter
in the sky.
He fires a cannonball at him.
He misses.

Peter takes Wendy and the boys
to his camp.
There are other boys there.
They call themselves the Lost Boys.

Peter and Wendy go
to see the mermaids.
Captain Hook is there.
He has Tiger Lily.

Hook ties Tiger Lily
to a rock.
He wants to know
where Peter lives.

Peter fights Hook.
Hook falls into the water.
The Croc is waiting.

Hook swims away.
Peter saves Tiger Lily.
He takes her home.

Tinker Bell is mad.
Peter is spending
too much time
with Wendy.

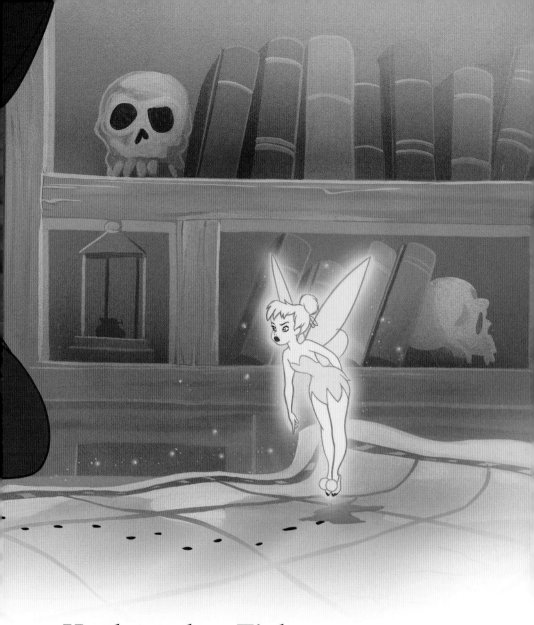

Hook catches Tink.
He says he will get rid of Wendy
if Tink tells him
where Peter lives.

Wendy likes Never Land,
but she misses home.
She tells Peter
it is time to go home.

The Lost Boys
want to go, too.
They leave Peter's hideout.
Hook is waiting.

Hook captures Wendy
and the boys.
He leaves a gift for Peter.
It is a bomb!

Tink comes just in time.
Hook tricked her.
She tells Peter
about the bomb.

Hook takes Wendy and the boys
to his ship.
He wants to make them pirates.

Wendy says no.
She knows Peter
will save them.

Hook is mad.
He makes Wendy
walk the plank.

Wendy jumps off the plank.

Peter is there.

He catches her!

Peter fights Hook.
The Lost Boys
fight the pirates.

Hook falls off the ship.
The Croc is
waiting for him!

Peter takes over the ship.
Now he is Captain Pan.
He takes Wendy
and the boys home.

Wendy says good-bye to Peter.
She loves Never Land,
but it is time
to grow up.